In loving memory
of my parents,
Carolynn and Lou.

Without whom CarLou
would not exist.

Published by CarLou Interactive Media and Publishing
www.carloumedia.com

Bella Wishes makes three wishes...

as she swings her hips to and fro.

She moves her hips to the left.

She swings her hips to the right.

She jumps high...

then she wiggles low.

Her face is covered with a
bright, pink veil.

The bells on her hips *ring, ring!*

She moves her hips to the left.
She swings her hips to the right.

She moves them all around,
swing, swing!

Bella jiggles...

then she giggles.

Her belly moves up...

and then down.

She moves her hips to the left.

She swings her hips to the right.

She always has a smile...

not a frown.

Her toes are tappin'...

Her fingers are snappin'.

Her leg kicks left...

and then right.

She swings to the left.
She jumps to the right.

Bella dances all day and all night.

Bella loves to dance.
Bella lives to prance.

She always has to be on the go.

She wiggles to the left.
She giggles to the right.

Her body jiggles 'round, high and low.

Bella Wishes makes three wishes

as she goes to sleep at night.

She wishes one swing to the left.
She wishes two swings to the right.

And on three swings, she spins
and says, "*Good Night!*"

About the Author:

Tessa May a.k.a. Tess Cacciatore is a long time entertainment industry veteran and an award-winning, multi-media writer and producer. A native of Des Moines, Iowa, Tess devotes much of her time to educating and empowering children. To date, her World Trust Foundation (www.worldtrust.org) has made a positive impact to thousands of children from many countries.

Tess has traveled the world capturing footage and photographs of children and indigenous peoples with the theme of building cross-cultural tolerance and understanding. Her content is being made into an interactive, educational series to bridge the youth of the world.

She now adds children's book author to her growing list of life achievements. Her first book, "Bella Wishes" is to instill a strong self-image for young girls, to have fun exercising with music and dance, and to feel confident about their bodies from an early age.

Tess currently resides in Los Angeles, CA. A portion of the proceeds will go to the **Youth Scholarship Fund** through the World Trust Foundation. tess@worldtrust.org.

About the Illustrator:

A native of New York, now living in Los Angeles, CA, **Dave Rodriguez** is a graduate of the California Institute of the Arts. Dave has developed his love for design into a successful career in animation. He has worked at major animation studios on a "who's who" list of shows including: The Ninja Turtles, The Rugrats, The Simpsons, Rocket Power, My Little Pony, Care Bears and Charlie Brown Specials, to name a few.

In addition to his busy career, David enjoys sharing his talents by volunteering his time with special projects. He has spoken to numerous high school audiences and participated in the Industry Education Council Career Conference. As a leading storyboard artist, Dave continues to enjoy the world of animation by developing and designing his own creations.

He is truly drawn to his field.

Bella Wishes™ says to make three wishes, and you too can own the following products soon to be released:

* *Bella Wishes*™ Plush Bella Doll

* *Bella Wishes*™ 30-minute belly dancing, exercise video/DVD, for hours of fun and dance.

* *Bella Wishes*™ Sing and Dance-Along CD.

You won't have to wait for the *Bella Wishes*™ Theme Song and Audio of the book.

Look in the back cover... it's there for you now!